DANIEL KIRK

YOU ARE NOT MY FRIEND, BUT I MISS YOU

Abrams Books for Young Readers
New York

To Rowan
—D. K.

The illustrations in this book were made with pen and ink,
which were then scanned, and color and texture were added digitally.

Library of Congress Cataloging-in-Publication Data

Kirk, Daniel, author, illustrator.
You are not my friend, but I miss you / Daniel Kirk.
pages cm
Summary: A sock monkey becomes angry with a stuffed dog while they
are playing and declares they are no longer friends, but soon learns
that he may not have been a good friend, either.
ISBN 978-1-4197-1236-4
[1. Friendship—Fiction. 2. Sharing—Fiction. 3. Toys—Fiction.] I. Title.
PZ7.K6339You 2014
[E]—dc23
2013041483

Text and illustrations copyright © 2014 Daniel Kirk
Book design by Chad W. Beckerman

Printed and bound in China
10 9 8 7 6 5 4 3 2 1

Abrams Books for Young Readers are available at special discounts when purchased
in quantity for premiums and promotions as well as fundraising or educational
use. Special editions can also be created to specification. For details, contact
specialsales@abramsbooks.com or the address below.

ABRAMS
THE ART OF BOOKS SINCE 1949

115 West 18th Street
New York, NY 10011
www.abramsbooks.com

You are not my friend.

Not anymore!

You took
my ball—

just like that!

You wouldn't give me my ball back.
You wouldn't share.

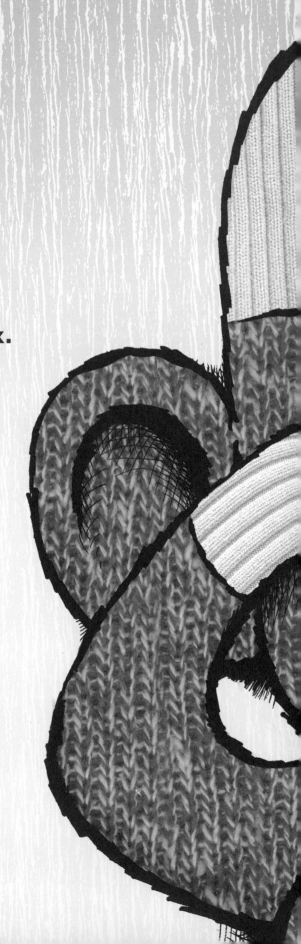

I had to grab it
when you weren't looking!

Now **I** have my ball,

and **YOU** cannot
play with it anymore!

YOU

cannot play with

ME.

Friends

are

supposed

to share.

I will find a **NEW** friend to play with.

This is

so much

fun.

Everybody needs a friend to share with.

Or . . .

maybe . . .

it isn't!

I know—I will play by myself!

I will be my own friend.

I will

share with

Still, I remember you
when I am
all
by
myself.

But I can be!
Will you come and play with me?

Maybe I didn't share.

Maybe **I** wasn't a great friend.

CATCH!